OBLIGATE SYNCHRONY

MATTHEW DYER

Obligate Synchrony

First edition

Printed in the United States of America

ISBN: 978-1-970775-03-7

LCCN: 2026904458

Published by Quiet Current Press

An imprint of Stratum Sphere LLC

Texas, United States

Written by Matthew Dyer

Cover design and interior design by the author.

File status: Archived.

CASE NO.   Experiment 717-Δ

OBLIGATE SYNCHRONY

NOTES:

PROTOCOL HEARINGS

Declassified from Administrative Vault H-7 / Experiment 717-Δ Authorization Record

Document Status: Partial reconstruction from mixed-media sources.

Integrity Rating: 0.82

**Gaps and redactions remain unrecovered.

HEARING LOG P-717Δ.01 — MANDATE CLARIFICATION

THE COMMITTEE CONVENED to define the operational language for Experiment 717-Δ.

The objective, as stated in the foundational charter, was to observe long-term evolutionary divergence between two interdependent biological constructs under controlled environmental constraints.

The term "**stability**" was formalized to mean:

> A condition in which system continuity is maintained, regardless of internal cost.

The term "**acceptable loss**" was codified as:

> Any reduction in population or complexity that does not compromise analytical clarity.

The term "**observer neutrality**" was adopted without definition.

The committee declined to specify its boundaries.

No dissent recorded.

HEARING LOG P-717Δ.03 — INTERVENTION POLICY DELIBERATION

THE COMMITTEE EXAMINED the question of potential intervention scenarios.

A note in the margin (author unspecified) states:

Intervention complicates attribution of causality.

A counter-note immediately beneath:

Non-intervention complicates attribution of responsibility.

The counter-note was struck through in a single motion.
The original wording remains legible in recovered scans.

The final protocol affirms:

Observers shall not intervene in organism-level processes.

Environmental regulation systems may self-correct to maintain experimental conditions, provided such corrections do not directly alter biological trajectories.

Mechanisms for determining what constitutes a "direct alteration" were tabled for future clarification.

No follow-up meeting appears in the record.

HEARING LOG P-717Δ.07 — DIVERGENCE CRITERIA

THE COMMITTEE DEBATED how to categorize evolutionary drift.

Early drafts proposed a three-tier system:

1. Identical Baseline
2. Minor Drift
3. Major Divergence

A later revision replaced "Major Divergence" with "Locked Trajectory", justified on the grounds that the latter term "carries no implicit value statement."

To maintain analytical clarity during divergence assessment, the committee confirmed that two parallel ecological containment units will be utilized.

Each unit will operate under identical baseline conditions with no cross-environment permeability.

This configuration ensures that any variants may develop without inter-lineage interference, thereby preserving the independence of observed evolutionary pathways.

Containment integrity will be monitored continuously, no exceptions to enclosure separation are permitted under Protocol 717-Δ.

A footnote, presumably from an external reviewer, queries

whether neutrality of terminology prevents ethical entanglement or merely conceals it.

This footnote is circled in red ink.

No committee response preserved.

HEARING LOG P-717Δ.09 — MORTALITY AS METRIC

A DISCUSSION AROSE REGARDING mortality tracking.
The finalized directive states:

Mortality events shall be treated as data points. Attribution of meaning to mortality lies outside experimental scope.

A supplemental clause was added emphasizing that losses occurring before the divergence threshold are to be considered "informationally negligible."

No definition provided for "negligible."

An unindexed voice in the background audio expresses concern about early extinctions within emergent sub-lineages. The concern was not incorporated into the minutes.

Its inclusion in this reconstruction is the result of high-gain archival enhancement.

HEARING LOG P-717Δ.12 — ETHICAL OVERSIGHT MANDATE

THE COMMITTEE FORMALIZED the requirement for an Ethical Observer.

Their function was defined as:

To record methodological tension without influencing experimental direction.

A second clause marked 'provisional' states:

Ethical record keeping is essential for audit purposes; the presence of ethical tension does not imply ethical authority.

The clause remains provisional in all surviving copies. No evidence exists of its ratification.

HEARING LOG P-717Δ.14 — FINAL AUTHORIZATION

EXPERIMENT 717-Δ RECEIVED UNANIMOUS APPROVAL.

A final note from the Oversight Chair summarizes the collective stance:

The system must reveal its own truths. Interference would distort what life selects for itself.

Beneath this, in handwriting that does not match any recorded signature:

Unless the truth is shaped by what we refuse to touch.

The handwritten line is partially obscured by water damage. No attribution possible.

ARCHIVE

This document contains the preserved observational materials from Experiment 717-Δ, an extended-duration evolutionary study involving two interdependent biological lineages provisionally designated PLANT and CREATURE. The intent of the archive is not to reconstruct events in narrative order, but to maintain fidelity to the record as it was produced across the experiment's active period.

Each entry appears in its original triptych format:

1. Archivist Log — empirical record, procedural in tone
2. Director Log — interpretive compression into stability frameworks

3. Ethicist Log — analytical tension regarding the
   implications of observer decisions

Terminology has remained unedited except where redaction
was required for continuity or legal compliance. Several intervals
in the archive include incomplete logs, missing attachments, or
irrecoverable data blocks. These omissions have been left visible,
as removal would interfere with historical integrity.

The experimental framework assumed:

- Two species whose survival depended on mutually
  exclusive resource production
- No permitted alteration of internal variables after
  initial conditions were established
- No corrective intervention within the biosphere
  except through observation
- External forces constrained to environmental drift and
  unavoidable systemic noise

All observer commentary reflects the perspective and limitations of its respective role. No unified interpretation should be inferred from their juxtaposition. Readers are advised that divergence among the three voices is a feature of the archive, not an error in compilation.

Where numerical summaries contradict qualitative observations, both have been retained. The archive's mandate is preservation, not adjudication.

The experiment concluded in accordance with institutional protocols. Its aftermath, and the status of surviving lineages, are documented in the final phase. This preface is not intended to guide interpretation, assign responsibility, or propose corrective measures. It serves only to introduce the structure as it stands:

incomplete, internally inconsistent, and unannotated beyond the minimal threshold required for comprehension.

All further meaning must be derived from the logs themselves.

———

Document ID: MAP/CONTAIN/717-Δ

[UNIT A — Containment Environment]

- Closed ecological chamber
- Standardized substrate and climate control
- No external biological input
- Barrier Layer: Composite-Seal 7C
- Interface Ports: Telemetric-only

|| BARRIER PERMEABILITY ≈ o ||
|| PHYSICAL ISOLATION SEALED ||
[UNIT B — Containment Environment]

- Closed ecological chamber
- Standardized substrate and climate control
- No external biological input
- Barrier Layer: Composite-Seal 7C
- Interface Ports: Telemetric-only

|| BARRIER PERMEABILITY ≈ o ||
|| PHYSICAL ISOLATION SEALED ||
NOTES:

- Units are synchronized in cycle timing and environmental modulation.
- All inter-unit pathways locked under Protocol 717-Δ.

- Direct comparison permitted only through remote data aggregation.

PHASE I
IDENTICAL BASELINE

SET 1 —
INITIAL STATE METRICS

ARCHIVIST LOG — P1.S1.A

TIMESTAMP: Cycle 0000.000 - 0000.047

Environmental constants remain unchanged since activation: uniform atmospheric saturation, mineral distribution consistent across substrate grids, thermal gradients minimal and evenly dispersed. No external pressures introduced. Under these conditions, both PLANT and CREATURE display indistinguishable metabolic sequences when reduced to exchange curves.

Resource Exchange Table, Initial:

- PLANT outputs Vapor-Nutrient A, absorbed by CREATURE integument without variation.
- CREATURE outputs Residue-Compound B, accumulated in soil strata and assimilated by PLANT root analogs.

Rates remain equal within error margins (<0.02%).

Early interactions present as symmetric loops: proximity-cohesion patterns, rhythmic release/uptake, mirrored cycles of metabolic quiet. No sign yet of preferential behavior.

A minor anomaly emerged in PLANT growth rates within Quadrant 4. Values exceeded baseline by 0.4%. Flagged as stochastic fluctuation; will continue monitoring. No functional interpretation assigned.

CREATURE clustering density shows slight drift (approximately. 1% increase within high-A zones). Again, treated as noise.

No detectable tensions within the system. No detectable intention. Only closed loops, unbroken.

End of Log.

———

DIRECTOR LOG — P1.S1.D

Summary Interval: Cycle 0000

Population models converge on stable equilibrium. Exchange rates display low-variance oscillation; no threat vectors identified. Energy costs minimal. Mortality during initialization $<0.1\%$ and consistent with activation norms.

Conditions are optimal for divergence observation. Stability here is not static but an economically neutral plateau—productive quiet before drift. No intervention required.

Proceed to extended monitoring.

End of Directive.

———

ETHICIST LOG — P1.S1.E

Cycle Reflection: oooo

Framework asserts the early state is neutral. I note that neutrality, in this context, is imposed. Neither PLANT nor CREATURE demonstrates capacity for deviation from the loop; their 'equilibrium' is less a balance than a binding.

If dependence exists before choice emerges, does that dependence carry meaning, or is meaning something we assign only after divergence?

The logs treat this state as beginning, but perhaps it is already a condition with cost—simply one we cannot yet measure.

End of Reflection.

DATAFRAG I.A — BASELINE SAMPLE SUMMARY (UNCOMPRESSED)

CYCLE: 0004.112 - 0004.350

ENV-A: Baseline metrics stabilized.
ENV-B: Baseline metrics stabilized.

PLANT_METRIC:
Membrane Density: 1.0004 ±0.0001
Output_A: 100% normalized
CREATURE_METRIC:
Uptake_B: 100% normalized

COHERENCE INDEX: 0.9998
NOISE_BANDWIDTH: <0.01%
ANOMALY: None detected

NOTES: System equilibrium stable. No deviation.

SET 2 — FOUNDATIONAL SYMMETRIES

ARCHIVIST LOG — P1.S2.A

TIMESTAMP: Cycle 0012.000 - 0012.983

Complete morphological mapping across twelve representative clusters. Key findings:

1. PLANT architecture exhibits consistent radial patterning. Root analogs form lattice structures around Residue-Compound B deposits, suggesting passive efficiency rather than behavioral seeking
2. CREATURE morphology remains uniformly soft-shelled, semi-permeable. Intake of Vapor-Nutrient A confirmed through surface-diffusion rather than discrete organs.

Early analyses categorize both species as metabolically identical in shape-adjacent efficiencies. But energy-trace imaging reveals faint discrepancies: CREATURE expenditure during Vapor-Nutrient absorption exceeds PLANT expenditure during Residue-Compound assimilation by approximately 3%. Too minor for functional significance; noted as preliminary irregularity.

Nutrient inefficiencies accumulating across cycles. Predominantly micro-scale: incomplete uptake, diffuse losses at boundary layers, decay residues. No explicit ecological consequence yet.

Patterns remain symmetric to the eye—mirror-like distributions across mapped quadrants. But symmetry often conceals drift until drift becomes visible.

Recording continues.

End of Log.

DIRECTOR LOG — P1.S2.D

Summary Interval: Cycle 0013

Inefficiencies catalogued by the Archivist ranked according to threat index. All fall within the lower two tiers. Projected long-term impact unlikely to alter macro-stability without amplification through external pressure.

Minor imbalances are not only tolerable but necessary. Without tension gradients, productive drift cannot occur. Categorize current deviations as useful precursors.

System behavior remains stable. Continue.

End of Directive.

ETHICIST LOG — P1.S2.E

Cycle Reflection: 0013

Imbalance becomes meaningful long before metrics acknowledge it. A 3% expenditure discrepancy may appear trivial, but meaning often precedes measurement.

Symmetry is declared when values fall within a chosen tolerance. If we altered the tolerance, the symmetry would vanish. Yet our logs will preserve the illusion until the illusion collapses.

I wonder if the first symmetry between the species is not in morphology or resource cost, but in the way we already discuss them.

End of Reflection.

FILE REF: OBS/PLANT-CREATURE/MORT.0007

STATUS: Unrecoverable

Metadata indicates this file once contained early-series mortality data for paired PLANT/CREATURE units.
    File header preserved; body content missing
    Checksum returns null value.
    Reason for loss: unknown.
    Retention directive: preserve empty shell.

SYSLOG-CONT.01 — CONTAINMENT BARRIER VERIFICATION

CYCLE: 0022.551

SUBSYSTEM: Environmental Containment Framework

Barrier Integrity (Unit A → Unit B): 100.0%

Barrier Integrity (Unit B → Unit A): 100.0%

Cross-Environment Permeability Test:

Molecular Transfer: 0.000

Volatile Exchange: 0.000

Biological Drift: 0.000

Calibration Notes: No cross-lineage migration pathways detected.

Conclusion: Containment units remain fully isolated.

End of SYSLOG.

SET 3 — ZERO-DIVERGENCE VERIFICATION

ARCHIVIST LOG — P1.S3.A

TIMESTAMP: Cycle 0025.041 - 0025.500

Full-system verification completed prior to divergence authorization.

Genetic drift within both species remains statistically minimal. No phenotypic deviations exceeding baseline noise. Exchange loops maintain mutual necessity without directional bias.

A small-scale mortality event occurred in PLANT samples within Quadrant 9. Rate: 0.7%. Necrotic tissue localized around low-B soil pockets. Treated as calibration artifact from earlier nutrient-distribution pulses. Samples removed; environment reset.

Snapshots taken, archived. No further structural anomalies identified.

With this, baseline period concludes.

End of Log.

DIRECTOR LOG — P1.S3.D

Summary Interval: Cycle 0025

Mortality event deemed statistically negligible. Impact modeling shows zero effect on broader stability metrics.

All indicators support transition to divergence phase. System stable, costs contained, populations suitable for evolutionary differentiation.

Authorize shift.

End of Directive.

ETHICIST LOG — P1.S3.E

Cycle Reflection: 0025

To categorize life loss as negligible is to reduce significance to fraction. Yet significance is not scalar. A life erased at the start may carry no recorded effects, but absence radiates through what could have occurred.

We prepare to watch species diverge. But what has disappeared already—quietly, early, without comment—may shape the ethics of every phase that follows.

Metrics may forget. Logs may minimize. But the archive itself remembers.

End of Reflection.

PHASE II

MICRO-DIVERGENCE

SET 4 —
VARIATION DRIFT NOTES

ARCHIVIST LOG — P2.S4.A

TIMESTAMP: Cycle 0032.110 - 0033.004

Micro-thickening observed along the PLANT outer membrane. Distinct from baseline: surface density increased by 1.7%, structure retains semi-permeability but shows faint curvature rigidity. Distribution uniform across sample groups, suggesting stable heritability rather than isolated mutation.

CREATURE morphology simultaneously presents extension in extraction appendage length. Increase varies between 2-4% across clusters. Preliminary modeling indicates enhanced reach during residue uptake but no measurable alteration in rate efficiency.

Both shifts appear independent yet temporally aligned. No functional consequences noted. Exchange loops remain intact; atmospheric saturation unchanged.

Described as early drift—subtle, nearly imperceptible. Not yet consequential.

Drift remains consistent within each isolated environment.

Comparative mapping across Units A and B shows no cross-environment influence.

End of Log.

DIRECTOR LOG — P2.S4.D

Summary Interval: Cycle 0033

Structural membrane changes in PLANT and appendage elongation in CREATURE fall squarely within the tolerances for adaptive noise. No alteration to survivability curves; no shift in projected equilibrium dynamics.

These variations require neither mitigation nor intervention. Categorize as drift-phase variability. Maintain standard monitoring cadence.

End of Directive.

ETHICIST LOG — P2.S4.E

Cycle Reflection: 0033

"Not yet consequential" can describe scale or perspective. The logs treat it as the former. I am less certain.

Changes this small rarely announce their future significance. Asymmetry, once introduced, has no natural impetus to reverse. We may already be watching divergence, simply at a resolution too narrow for certainty.

By the time consequence becomes measurable, the cost of reversal may be impossible.

End of Reflection.

DATAFRAG II.Δ — VARIANCE SCAN (UNRESOLVED)

CYCLE: 0034.009

SCAN_MODES: Structural / Metabolic / Resonance
    RESULT:
    PLANT_OUTER_THICKENING: +1.7%
    CREATURE_EXTRACTION_LEN: +3.1%
    Energy Drift (micro): 0.43%
    TEMPORAL HARMONIC:
    3-peak alignment at $\Delta t = 0.12, 0.24, 0.36$ s
    FLAGGED_AS: Statistical Noise

FILE REF: VAR/DRIFT-SEQ/Δ-02

STATUS: Partial Corruption

Contents beyond timestamp marker cannot be reconstructed.

Fragmented remnants suggest environmental drift measurements outside normal tolerance. Information insufficient for reassembly.

Archivist note: entry retained in damaged state to preserve continuity of sequence.

SET 5 —
SELECTIVE EDGES

ARCHIVIST LOG — P2.S5.A

TIMESTAMP: Cycle 0041.009 - 0042.775

Early mutation clusters demonstrate coupled progression:

1. PLANT samples now produce detectable traces of Bitter Compound C. Concentration low—0.03% increase in chemical complexity—but sufficient to alter CREATURE uptake behavior during testing intervals.
2. CREATURE samples show elevated tolerance thresholds. Surface receptors adjust uptake rates to counteract the compound's inhibitory effects.

Laboratory mortality rates rise modestly among CREATURE individuals lacking tolerance adaptation. Decrease also observed among PLANT individuals whose compound production lags behind population mean. No cross-species mortality detected.

The paired emergence of compound and tolerance forms a selective edge: discrete advantages only in combination.

As before, interaction loops remain functional.

End of Log.

DIRECTOR LOG — P2.S5.D

Summary Interval: Cycle 0042

The mortality increase aligns with expected patterns of productive culling during adaptive edge formation. Non-tolerant CREATURE individuals and sub-threshold PLANT producers represent disadvantageous outliers that would destabilize long-term drift if retained.

This is the measurable onset of divergence. It is appropriate and necessary. Approve continued monitoring without correction.

End of Directive.

ETHICIST LOG — P2.S5.E

Cycle Reflection: 0042

"Productive culling" suggests utility where there is loss. Mortality becomes a mechanism rather than an outcome. It reframes harm as optimization.

The language is efficient, but efficiency often conceals its own premises.

Selection may be inevitable within the system, but inevitability does not erase cost. The individuals who fail to adapt do not vanish cleanly; they simply vanish quietly.

The logs will remember the shift but not the ones who marked its threshold.

End of Reflection.

SYSLOG-ENV.01 — BASELINE CALIBRATION DRIFT

CYCLE: 0049.220

SUBSYSTEM: Environmental Regulation Array

Calibration drift detected in Thermal Modulation Unit 3.

Variation: +0.14°C above predicted tolerance.

Feedback loop auto-corrected after 0.7 seconds.

Secondary anomaly: low-amplitude harmonic oscillation observed in Sensor Channel 4 during correction cycle.

Frequency band: 11.2-11.4 Hz.

Classified as benign electrical resonance artifact.

No biological system alerted.

No further action required.

End of SYSLOG.

SET 6 —
IRREVERSIBLE MINORITIES

ARCHIVIST LOG — P2.S6.A

TIMESTAMP: Cycle 0054.330 - 0055.112

A small PLANT lineage, <4% of total population, has developed irregular signaling pulses—brief electromagnetic fluctuations along membrane ridges. No functional effect observed on uptake or growth cycles. Pulses appear stochastic, though patterns may emerge with further data.

Parallel to this, a CREATURE sub-lineage expresses subtle early specialization: restructuring of internal diffusion paths that improve efficiency of Vapor-Nutrient A absorption by 6%. However, this comes at the expense of sensory range; these individuals respond sluggishly to environmental shifts.

Neither lineage exhibits strong reproductive persistence. Both remain stable but numerically marginal.

Noted as minor branches. Trajectories uncertain.

End of Log.

DIRECTOR LOG — P2.S6.D

Summary Interval: Cycle 0055

Branches that fail to propagate effectively qualify as inefficient forks. Their persistence offers little value in modeling long-term dynamics.

An algorithm recommending accelerated environmental stress conditions is prepared to test resilience across all minority lineages. Stress will clarify functional utility and eliminate noise.

Proceed pending approval.

End of Directive.

ETHICIST LOG — P2.S6.E

Cycle Reflection: 0055

The proposal for accelerated stress prompts unease I cannot fully articulate within procedural vocabulary. The intent is measurement, not harm, yet harm may occur regardless of intent.

If a lineage disappears because the environment shifted too quickly for adaptation, is that an observation or an imposition? If we create the conditions under which loss becomes inevitable, does our neutrality remain intact?

I cannot answer. I can only record the hesitation.

End of Reflection.

MEMO 1 — RESOURCE ALLOCATION INQUIRY

DOCUMENT ID: ADMIN/OPS-RQ/Δ72
Recipient: Experiment 717-Δ Oversight Cluster
Subject: Projected Energy Draw Increase

Energy consumption models indicate a 9-14% increase in system load over the next seven cycles due to expanded defensive-expression mapping in biological subsystems.

Request clarification on whether additional funding requisition is permitted or whether non-critical monitoring arrays should be temporarily suspended to maintain budget compliance.

Note: Suspension of peripheral arrays is not expected to affect primary dataset integrity.
Potential impact on rare or low-frequency phenomena remains unquantified.

Awaiting directive.
—Administrative Liaison Unit

PHASE III

EARLY CO-ESCALATORY MORPHOLOGY VS RECIPROCAL CALIBRATION

FILE REF: SIG/IRR-PULSE/REC-14

STATUS: Redacted Prior to Preservation

Only first 26 characters recoverable:

Initial pulse pattern suggests—

Remaining 89% of document removed under Protocol Ω-Redact.

Redaction authorization source unlisted.

File preserved in altered form.

SET 7 — FIRST DIVERGING PATHWAYS

ARCHIVIST LOG — P3.S7.A

TIMESTAMP: Cycle 0071.004 - 0072.889

The PLANT population contained in Unit A demonstrates measurable increases in toxin precursor compounds—primarily pro-reactive molecules accumulating in outer membrane micro-chambers. Concentrations remain below active toxicity thresholds but clearly trend upward.

The PLANT population contained in Unit B exhibit an opposite adaptation: emergence of glandular exudates along ridged surfaces. These exudates soften membrane texture and ease CREATURE extraction, reducing mechanical stress during contact by a documented 12%.

CREATURE lineages reflect a similar split. Unit A individuals have developed sharper extraction tools in the form of keratinized points capable of piercing early-stage PLANT defenses. Unit B individuals exhibit narrowing at the feeding interface, allowing for precision uptake with minimal tissue disruption.

These patterns rise in parallel. Early evidence indicates two distinct evolutionary trajectories forming within otherwise identical environmental conditions. No direct interference yet identified.

Both trajectories remain viable. Their stability remains untested.

End of Log.

DIRECTOR LOG — P3.S7.D

Summary Interval: Cycle 0072

The emergent traits categorize cleanly into two strategic modes:

1. Competitive Strategy
   - PLANT toxin precursor accumulation
   - CREATURE sharp-tool extraction
2. Cooperative Strategy
   - PLANT glandular exudates
   - CREATURE precision feeding apparatus

Model projections indicate the Competitive Strategy will dominate under any measurable pressure scenario due to faster response scaling and superior short-term resilience.

Both modes will be permitted to continue. Observation will confirm relative viability.

End of Directive.

ETHICIST LOG — P3.S7.E

Cycle Reflection: 0072

Cooperation here is not a reduction of harm but an intentional exposure to it. To ease extraction is to accept vulnerability. To feed with precision is to gamble on trust that cannot be reciprocally proven.

The system rewards resilience; resilience is easier to achieve by resisting rather than yielding.

I wonder whether a cooperative lineage can survive when its survival depends on staying open in a world that increasingly closes.

End of Reflection.

DATAFRAG III.Ω — PARALLEL TRAIT PROJECTION MATRIX

CYCLE: 0078.200

ENV-A: Trait escalation above model expectation.
    ENV-B: Trait refinement persists under low variance.

BRANCH_A:
    Toxin_Precursor_C: ↑↑ (rate: 0.021/cycle)
    Extraction_ToolSharpness: ↑ (variable)
    Damage_Inflicted: +14%

BRANCH_B:
    Exudate_Smoothing: ↑↑ (rate: 0.017/cycle)
    Precision_Feeding_Index: +11%
    Damage_Inflicted: -22%

SEPARATION METRIC: 0.41 → 0.56

NOTES: Early divergence not yet classified as terminal.

SET 8 —
ESCALATING INTERFACES

ARCHIVIST LOG — P3.S8.A

TIMESTAMP: Cycle 0083.115 - 0085.022

Toxin variants are now diversifying. Unit A PLANT competitive-line individuals synthesize at least three early-stage compounds with differing volatility. Defensive layering increases—membrane thickening coupled with rapid closure reflexes during CREATURE approach.

Unit A CREATURE competitive-line extracts grow more specialized, developing dual-edge structures capable of breaching layered defenses. Increased tissue tearing observed at contact sites, though feeding efficiency rises.

In contrast, Unit B cooperative pairs show refinement: PLANT exudates now form smooth gradients around glandular ridges, while CREATURE precision feeders align extraction paths to avoid damaging key nutrient channels. Tissue damage reduced by an additional 8% compared to other earlier cycles.

Both strategies deepen. Interactions diverge. No cross-strategy pairings observed.

These remain early-stage interfaces, but the trajectories are unmistakable.

End of Log.

DIRECTOR LOG — P3.S8.D

Summary Interval: Cycle 0085

Cooperative success is attributable to cost-saving feedback loops: reduced tissue damage decrease repair energy expenditure for PLANT, while precision uptake reduces waste for CREATURE.

Despite this, projections show these mutualistic lineages are resource-sensitive and require stable surroundings for long-term persistence. Any disruption increases failure probability.

Competitive branches demonstrate greater robustness under stress scenarios. Their cost structures, while higher, produce resilience advantages.

No intervention warranted. Continue monitoring both interfaces.

End of Directive.

ETHICIST LOG — P3.S8.E

Cycle Reflection: 0085

If a cooperative lineage requires stability, does that signify weakness or worth? Fragility is often framed as inefficiency, but fragility also signals the presence of something that cannot replace itself easily.

Where competition multiplies its strategies, cooperation depends on maintaining an opening that could always be exploited.

Perhaps its need for stability is not a deficit but a marker of a different kind of value—one that the system, as designed, is not inclined to measure.

End of Reflection.

FILE REF:
DIR/DRAFT-P3.S8.X

STATUS: Deleted; Partial Ghost Reconstruction

Reconstruction reveals fragmentary phrases:

...cooperative trend not... statistically negligible... reconsider classification...

No full sentences recoverable.
Deletion timestamp predates final Director log by < 1 cycle.
No explanation recorded.

SYSLOG-ENV.04 — SIGNAL COHERENCE FLAG

CYCLE: 0089.773
SUBSYSTEM: Multimodal Sensor Array

Unexpected signal coherence detected across Pulse-Spectrum Channels 4, 6, and 7.

Duration: 2.8 seconds

Pattern: Repeating interval of 0.42 seconds between peak alignments.

Correlation rating: 0.31 (below significance threshold).

FLAGGED_AS: Multi-channel noise artifact, likely induced by substrate vibration or sub-grid static buildup.

Logged for completeness only.
End of SYSLOG.

SET 9 —
BIFURCATION THRESHOLD

ARCHIVIST LOG — P3.S9.A
TIMESTAMP: Cycle 0099.004 - 0100.771

Long-form reproductive mapping confirms that the two Units have now diverged beyond the point of cross-interpretive equivalence.

Unit A populations exhibit sustained reinforcement of escalation-associated traits. Individuals lacking these traits show markedly reduced reproductive success, and no stabilizing-pattern variants persist at measurable representation.

Unit B populations display consistent progression toward interface-stabilizing traits. Escalation-pattern variants appear in early cycles but fail to persist and do not contribute to long-term lineage continuation.

This marks the formal bifurcation threshold:
    each Unit now maintains a single dominant evolutionary

trajectory, with no remaining internal variation capable of reversing direction.

Mortality in Unit A remains elevated due to metabolic burden associated with reinforcement traits.
Unit B maintains low mortality but limited expansion rate.

Two distinct paths now unfold separately:
one through increasing expenditure,
one through sustained mutual calibration.
End of Log.

DIRECTOR LOG — P3.S9.D

Summary Interval: Cycle 0100

Unit A continues refinement through high-cost expenditure cycles, eliminating inefficient forms. Stress simulations project long-term dominance of this trajectory under volatile conditions.

Unit B's trajectory remains viable only within narrow stability intervals, limiting scalability and resilience under projected fluctuations.

Observational stance unchanged.
Each Unit should be allowed to proceed along its established path.

End of Directive.

ETHICIST LOG — P3.S9.E

Cycle Reflection: 0100

Endurance interpreted as superiority disregards the cost of endurance. Unit A persists by escalating harm; Unit B persists by reducing it. Neither path is neutral.

The trajectory separation is irreversible now. Our decision to watch rather than redirect remains unacknowledged in the formal record.

Observation proceeds.

Observation does not separate us from consequences that accompany it.

End of Reflection.

FILE REF:
SYS/ENV/SEQ-099-102

STATUS: Sequence Gap

SYSLOG records for cycles 099.442 through 102.003 missing from registry.

Gap unexplained; upstream storage registers no associated error.

Absence noted but not investigated during original cycle.

Archive retains gap for accuracy.

MEMO 2 — PERSONNEL BEHAVIOR FLAG

DOCUMENT ID: HR/OBS-Flag/K-Δ

Recipient: Oversight Cluster, Behavioral Compliance

Subject: Observer Deviations from Procedural Distance

Routine behavioral audit detected the following:

- Archivist unit has accessed historical divergence case studies outside required reading.
- Query logs show increased searches related to "variance thresholds" and "early-stage collapse indicators."
- No procedural violations noted, but pattern suggests potential affective drift toward subject entities.

Recommended Action: Standard language reminder on observational neutrality.

No disciplinary action required at this time.

Flag set to passive monitoring.

—Personnel Oversight Node

PHASE IV
LOCKED TRAJECTORIES

SET 10 —
STABILITY COMPRESSION
REVIEW

ARCHIVIST LOG — P4.S10.A

TIMESTAMP: Cycle 0112.300 - 0114.991

Trait development in the two containment environments continues to diverge along established trajectories.

Unit A PLANT lineage exhibits fixation of escalation-associated traits.

Observed features include:

- Progressive membrane densification
- Multi-chamber toxin storage
- Rapid construction of resource-access channels in response to contact stimuli

Maintenance of these traits imposes sustained metabolic load.

Daily expenditure allocated to reinforcement and tissue turnover now averages 19%.

Despite the cost, these traits persist across reproductive cycles, indicating stabilization rather than temporary response.

Corresponding CREATURE traits in Unit A display comparable fixation patterns.

Observed features include:

- Incremental hardening of extraction appendages, with layers mineral deposition increasing structural rigidity
- Enhanced penetration dynamics, yielding greater force concentration at contact points
- Accelerated reflex arcs tied to resource acquisition, reducing the interval between detection and extraction attempts

Maintenance of these traits imposes significant energetic demand.

Metabolic modeling estimates that 11-15% of daily expenditure is allocated to reinforcement cycles, micro fracture repair, and structural mineral turnover.

Despite this cost burden, the traits persist with high fidelity across reproductive sequences, indicating long-term stabilization rather than transient escalation.

Unit B PLANT lineage traits continue to consolidate around stabilization and synchronized exchange.

Observed features include:

- Regulated exudate cycling, with secretion intervals increasingly aligned to CREATURE feeding rhythms
- Reduced defensive activation, indicated by lower incidence of reflexive constriction or barrier-thickening during CREATURE contact

- Nutrient channel dilation, maintaining consistent flow
  rates and minimizing localized tissue stress during
  resource transfer

Metabolic analysis shows that these traits flatten expenditure curves, reducing peak output demands and distributing energy use across predictable exchange windows.

Variance reduction aligns with measured decrease in CREATURE-side intake fluctuations, indicating bidirectional entrainment rather than isolated adaptation.

Trait persistence across reproductive cycles suggests increasing fixation of low-conflict, timing-dependent resource exchange, with no measurable tendency toward escalation behaviors or defensive reactivation.

Corresponding CREATURE traits in Unit B exhibit refinement toward reduced-impact acquisition behaviors.

Observed features include:

- Micro-modulated feeding appendages capable of
  adjusting pressure and flow rate to match PLANT
  exudate release curves
- Delayed-initiation reflexes, decreasing premature
  contact and lowering tissue disruption at exchange
  interfaces
- Rhythmic intake calibration, coordinating resource
  uptake with PLANT metabolic recovery intervals

Energetic modeling indicates that these traits reduce variance in daily expenditure, distribution metabolic load across predictable cycles rather than abrupt surges.

Estimated efficiency gains remain aligned with PLANT-side improvements (~14%), reflecting bidirectional synchronization rather than unilateral adaptation.

Trait persistence across reproductive sequences suggests fixation toward low-damage, timing-dependent resource exchange, with no evidence of reversion toward earlier, higher-impact extraction behaviors.

Each Unit now maintains a distinct ecological pattern:

Unit A operates under continuous micro-conflict dynamics; Unit B under tightly synchronized exchange dynamics.

No evidence suggests reversibility toward earlier, undifferentiated states.

End of Log.

DIRECTOR LOG — P4.S10.D

Summary Interval: Cycle 0115

Unit A's expenditure-intensive trait set remains consistent with evolutionarily honest escalation: costly traits persist because they provide repeatable advantages under competitive pressure. High maintenance load is acceptable within this evaluative framework.

Unit B's trajectory maintains stability through reciprocal timing and resource coordination. Such equilibrium is contingent upon precise mutual dependency and therefore exhibits characteristics of artificial stability.

Resilience remains limited outside narrow environmental parameters.

Both trajectories remain viable at present.

Unit A retains priority in projected stress-adaptation models.

End of Directive.

ETHICIST LOG — P4.S10.E

Cycle Reflection: 0115

Honesty seems an unusual term for escalation.

If increased cost and increased harm define honest adaptation, then stabilizing traits become excluded by definition.

Unit B's stability is labeled artificial because it requires coordination and restraint—forms of dependency that do not resemble dominance.

This may be why such dependency is treated as suspect: resilience is prioritized over relational cost.

Interpretations diverge as sharply as the Units themselves.

The species do not provide commentary; the observers do.

End of Reflection.

FILE REF: VID/TRP-RESP/ECO-412

STATUS: Data Block Failure

Visual record of first reflexive trap response failed storage verification.

Captured frames unrecoverable.

Audio track blank.

Technician note appended:

____

System stable. Re-run unnecessary.

____

File retained as empty placeholder.

DATAFRAG IV.B — TRAIT FIXATION AUDIT (PARTIAL)

CYCLE: 0121.991

COMPETITIVE_TRAITS:

Membrane_Ossification: 89% lineage saturation

Reflexive_Trap_Response: <0.3s latency

Metabolic_Cost: +19%

COOPERATIVE_TRAITS:

Sync_Rhythm_Alignment: 0.82 coherence

Shared_Matrix_Integrity: 76%

Regenerative_Cost: -9%

CROSS-VIABILITY SCORE: 2.1% (trend: ↓)

SET 11 —
FEEDBACK SATURATION

ARCHIVIST LOG — P4.S11.A
TIMESTAMP: Cycle 0126.044 - 0127.818

CREATURE individuals within Unit A now demonstrate stealth-feeding behavior: reduced thermal footprint, slowed approach vectors, and low-noise membrane contact.

PLANT defensive structures respond with rapid trap reflexes—sub-second closure of membrane folds capable of temporarily immobilizing smaller CREATURE individuals.

Mortality events increase slightly in both populations during these interactions. Energy cost of repeated stealth attempts and trap activations contributes to further attrition.

Within Unit B lineages, shared structures begin forming—thin, semi-permeable connective matrices bridging PLANT and CREATURE bodies at consistent intervals. These matrices reduce energy cost by redistributing nutrient transport load across shared tissue. Early dissolution sequences ensure separation when one partner enters temporary dormancy.

Both systems are intensifying along their respective paths. Reversal less likely with each cycle.

End of Log.

DIRECTOR LOG — P4.S11.D

Summary Interval: Cycle 0128

The connective matrices observed in Unit B lineages constitute structural inefficiencies anesthetized by familiarity. They reduce cost internally but increase reliance on partner stability, creating vulnerability to unilateral failure.

Unit B's low mortality profile produces false positives of success: survivability metrics appear favorable only because stressors remain minimal. Models predict significant fragility under any sharp environmental fluctuation.

By contrast, Unit A branches maintain higher baseline attrition but produce individuals robust under escalating feedback loops.

Continue observations. No corrective action required.

End of Directive.

ETHICIST LOG — P4.S11.E

Cycle Reflection: 0128

"False positives of success" is a difficult phrase to read. If low mortality cannot be considered success, the criteria being used may no longer reflect anything intrinsic to the organisms themselves.

Shared structures are interpreted as inefficiencies, yet their formation reduces harm and distributes cost. The competitive traits reduce neither.

Success, in these logs, has become synonymous with enduring pressure rather than reducing suffering. I question what kind of definition can hold that framing without distortion.

End of Reflection.

SYSLOG-ENV.07 — RECURSIVE PATTERN TRACE

CYCLE: 0137.441

SUBSYSTEM: Electromagnetic Field Mapping Layer

Low-level recursive pattern detected across EMF Ridge Sensors 2-5.

Detected form: nested waveform repetitions with diminishing amplitude.

Model fit returned no matching database signatures.

Classified as unstructured environmental interference.

Signal decayed without intervention.

No system components affected.

End of SYSLOG.

SET 12 —
POINT OF NO RETURN

ARCHIVIST LOG — P4.S12.A

TIMESTAMP: Cycle 0142.119 - 0144.050

Unit A ecosystem now operates under constant low-level attrition. Defensive structures degrade through repeated activation, requiring near-continuous regeneration. CREATURE extraction tools fracture, regrow, and resharpen in rapid cycles. Mortality remains steady but non-catastrophic, creating a dynamic equilibrium based on persistent loss.

Unit B ecosystems exhibit a different instability: collapse cascades occur when either PLANT or CREATURE fails to meet synchronized exchange thresholds. A missed cycle results in localized breakdown of shared tissues, then starvation feedback, then systemic failure. Yet when synchronization is maintained, these ecosystems achieve exceptionally high efficiency.

Neither system can revert. Both trajectories are fully locked.
    End of Log.

DIRECTOR LOG — P4.S12.D

Summary Interval: Cycle 0144

Both trajectories exhibit stably predictable outcomes:

- High-attrition competitive systems maintain resilience by continuous turnover.
- High-fragility cooperative systems maintain efficiency only when dependency remains intact.

These represent alternate expressions of the same underlying principle: dependency—on defense or on coordination—drives trajectory stability.

No further evaluation needed. Proceed with ongoing environmental neutrality.
End of Directive.

ETHICIST LOG — P4.S12.E

Cycle Reflection: 0144

Predictable does not mean acceptable, but the terms seem to be merging within the Director's framework. Stability, once quantified, becomes a justification for allowing conditions to persist unchanged.

The cooperative system's fragility is inseparable from trust—each partner relying on the other's consistent restraint. The competitive system's attrition is inseparable from domination—each partner protecting itself through increased harm to the other.

Both persist because we allow them to.

I record these distinctions, though I am unsure whether recording is enough.

End of Reflection.

MEMO 3 — PREDICTIVE MODEL DISCREPANCY

DOCUMENT ID: SIM/PRED-Revision/Δ217

Recipient: Director's Office

Subject: Divergence Between Predictive and Emergent Behavior Patterns

Simulation models for Unit A aggression vectors have begun diverging from real-time observation outcomes.

Observed escalation exceeds projected limits by 17%.

Additionally, Unit B survival rates remain above model predictions under moderate volatility, contradicting expected early-cycle collapse.

Recommendation:

- Update predictive curve fits to accommodate deviation
- Flag emergent behavior for review

Addendum: Analyst notes uncertainty whether deviations represent biological innovation or environmental modeling error.

No formal conclusion.

—Systems Prediction Division

MEMO 4 —
ENVIRONMENTAL
SYSTEMS
INTEGRITY NOTE

DOCUMENT ID: ENV/Σ-Fluctuation Report
Recipient: Infrastructure Maintenance Group
Subject: Non-Periodic Temperature Variance

Temperature modulation array recorded non-periodic fluctuation outside scheduled calibration cycles.
Magnitude within tolerance but anomalous in timing.

Cause unidentified.
Environmental controllers report no malfunction.

Recommend logging the event as systemic noise unless recurrence exceeds threshold frequency.

No action requested unless variance escalates.

—Environmental Regulation Sub-Unit

PHASE V
PRESSURE EVENT

SYSLOG-Δ.02 — VOLATILITY SPIKE DIAGNOSTICS

CYCLE: 0158.991

SUBSYSTEM: Crisis-Event Monitor (Δ-Channel)

Impacted environments: Unit A and Unit B.

Temperature variance exceeded model tolerance by +17.3%.

Source indeterminate. No internal malfunction detected.

External source probability: <1%.

Classified as emergent environmental fluctuation.

Concurrent anomaly: coherence in EMF Channels 3 and 4 forming linear ramp pattern.

Duration: 0.9 seconds.

Evaluated as non-hazardous.

System remains operational.

End of SYSLOG.

SET 13 — EMERGENT CONDITION Δ

ARCHIVIST LOG — P5.S13.A

TIMESTAMP: Cycle 0158.002 - 0159.661

A temperature volatility spike has appeared across all monitored quadrants. Variability exceeds predictive models by 17.3%. No correlation found within internal system cycles; classified as Emergent Condition Δ. No intervention enacted.

Unit A lineages exhibit hyper-defensive overexertion. PLANT segments activate toxin reservoirs continuously, bypassing normal modulation cycles. CREATURE competitive-line individuals respond with accelerated stealth-feeding attempts, increasing metabolic strain.

Unit B lineages show immediate reductions in coordination rate; exudate timing becomes irregular, and shared structures contract prematurely.

Both systems display stress signatures, but patterns differ sharply: escalation versus deceleration.

End of Log.

DIRECTOR LOG — P5.S13.D

Summary Interval: Cycle 0159

Emergent Condition Δ introduces necessary volatility for distinguishing robustness differential. Early indicators confirm that Unit A lineages possess higher resistance to shock variability, though at significant energy cost.

Unit B lineages show instability under the new temperature variance; predictive models estimate high die-off probability absent stabilization.

Observation continues. No corrective actions warranted.
End of Directive.

ETHICIST LOG — P5.S13.E

Cycle Reflection: 0159

Robustness is being treated as synonymous with worth. Yet robustness merely describes endurance under change, not the intrinsic value of the lineage that endures or fails.

Emergent Condition Δ arrived without intention. The interpretation we apply to its effects is entirely chosen. What we decide to label as meaningful will shape what survives, whether or not it was ever the system's purpose.
End of Reflection.

DATAFRAG V.Δ — VOLATILITY REACTION SNAPSHOT

CYCLE: 0164.511

ENV-A: Collapse events ↑ ↑ under toxin saturation.
ENV-B: Sync disruption recoverable within $\Delta t = 12.1s$.

ENVIRONMENT:
Temperature Variance Spike: +17.3%
Modulation_Lag: 0.8s

UNIT_A MEASURES:
Toxin Reservoir Saturation: 146% (critical)
Tool Integrity: Fracture Points ↑ ↑
Collapse Events: +38% (cycle-local)

UNIT_B MEASURES:
Sync_Disruption: 0.27 (temporary)
Matrix_Thinning: 41%
Regained Functionality: 63% after $\Delta t = 12.1s$

FLAGGED_AS: Event classified as uncontrolled variability.

SYSLOG-Δ.09 — PERSISTENT CROSS-CHANNEL CONVERGENCE

CYCLE: 0169.552
SUBSYSTEM: Emergency Stabilization Framework

Cross-channel convergence detected across Sensors 2-8.
Seven consecutive intervals showing recursive peak alignment.
Amplitude below intervention threshold.
Classification: non-critical anomaly.

Note: Pattern exhibited increasing regularity prior to dissipation.
Rate of convergence: 0.03 seconds per cycle shortening.
Final state: abrupt cessation without decay curve.

No operational compromise recorded.
End of SYSLOG.

SET 14 —
CASCADE ANALYSIS

ARCHIVIST LOG — P5.S14.A

TIMESTAMP: Cycle 0168.300 - 0170.044

Unit A PLANT lineages demonstrate widespread autolysis. Excessive toxin accumulation—triggered by continuous activation under Δ-variant volatility—causes membrane collapse and internal ruptures. Mortality spikes by 38%. Unit A CREATURE individuals show extraction-tool fragmentation and organ-level fatigue. Their feeding attempts increase in aggression as volatility continues.

Unit B lineage pairs experience near-collapse but maintain minimal functionality. Shared structures thin to almost transparent matrices; exudate rhythms falter but do not cease. CREATURE precision feeders reduce intake voluntarily, possibly as a passive mechanism to avoid system overload. PLANT partners retain partial metabolic coordination.

Total functional loss within mutualistic quadrants is significant but not absolute.

End of Log.

DIRECTOR LOG — P5.S14.D

Summary Interval: Cycle 0170

The collapse of toxin-heavy PLANT branches represents inefficient redundancy purged under destabilizing conditions. Competitive CREATURE mortality is substantial but consistent with a system clearing over-extended traits.

Cooperative-line survival at minimal levels demonstrated non-scalable persistence: functional enough to endure but insufficient to expand meaningfully. Such survival is constrained, not adaptive.

Overall, Emergent Condition Δ continues to produce clarifying results.

End of Directive.

ETHICIST LOG — P5.S14.E

Cycle Reflection: 0170

The distinction between "survival" and "being allowed to survive" becomes acute here. Competitive collapse is framed as necessary purification. Cooperative persistence is framed as failure to scale. Both interpretations shape future acceptability.

If Emergent Condition Δ exposes anything, it may not be the organisms but the architecture of our expectations—what we call efficient, valuable, viable.

The system changes. Our framing does not.
End of Reflection.

SYSLOG–Δ.12 — POST-VOLATILITY RESIDUAL TRACE

CYCLE: 0182.110

SUBSYSTEM: Δ-Resolution Audit

Residual trace detected in EMF logs following Δ stabilization.

Pattern is low amplitude, non-periodic, and partially corrupted.

Checksum returns as incomplete sequence.

Trace left unprocessed due to insufficient structure for meaningful compression.

Event archived without analysis.

End of SYSLOG.

SET 15 —
RESIDUAL SURVIVORS

ARCHIVIST LOG — P5.S15.A

TIMESTAMP: Cycle 0181.020 - 0183.903

Residual populations emerge post-Δ stabilization. Only a fraction remains in each Unit environment.

Unit A PLANT surviving lineage retains hardened structures but exhibit reduced toxin reservoirs. CREATURE surviving lineage displays more brittle extraction tools. Their aggression remains pronounced, though energy reserves are notably depleted.

Unit B surviving lineages maintain vestiges of shared tissue networks. Though weakened, these connections retain enough structural integrity to permit regeneration once environmental volatility decreases. Synchronization remains impaired but recoverable.

Residual populations reflect both loss and persistence. No further collapse observed.

End of Log.

DIRECTOR LOG — P5.S15.D

Summary Interval: Cycle 0184

Mutualistic survivors demonstrate resource-thrifty behavior but remain strategically brittle. Their reliance on coordinated exchange limits scalability under fluctuating conditions.

Competitive survivors, though weakened, retain directionally sound traits: defensive escalation and opportunistic extraction continue to provide clear survival trajectories.

Both lineages remain viable, though competitive systems maintain the more adaptable long-term posture.
End of Directive.

ETHICIST LOG — P5.S15.E

Cycle Reflection: 0184

The Director's framing reveals a contradiction: one lineage is "brittle but surviving," the other "directionally sound but collapsing." If success is defined by endurance, neither fully qualifies; if defined by regeneration, one clearly does.

I am left wondering what criteria are being optimized, and whether those criteria are aligned with the system as it is, or with the outcomes the observers expect to see.

Interpretation is not neutral. Residual survivors exist, but what we decide they represent will shape everything that follows.
End of Reflection.

MEMO 5 — PROTOCOL AUDIT REQUEST

DOCUMENT ID: ETH/Audit-Req/Δ-PostEvent
Recipient: Ethics Review Subcommittee
Subject: Clarification on Intervention Criteria

Following Emergent Condition Δ, a request has been submitted (origin unclear) regarding intervention definitions in high-volatility scenarios.

Existing protocol states:

- Intervention prohibited if it directly alters organism-level trajectories.
- Environmental recalibration permitted only to maintain baseline conditions.

Uncertainty has arisen regarding whether Δ qualifies as baseline deviation or novel state.

Request:

- Provide definition of "baseline" in contexts involving unmodeled environmental variance.
- Confirm whether failure to clarify constitutes implicit non-intervention directive.

Pending response.

—Ethics Liaison Unit

INTERVENTION CRISIS

SET 16 — OBSERVER TENSION METRICS

ARCHIVIST LOG — P6.S16.A

TIMESTAMP: Cycle 0197.004 - 0199.771

The gap between data and interpretation widens. Recorded values continue to quantify metabolic strain, lineage decline, and adaptive stalling, but the models increasingly fail to capture the lived dynamics within the populations. The dataset remains orderly; the implications do not.

A request—sender unidentified—has been logged for intervention modeling modules. The request did not specify intended scope. It has been archived as Protocol Query No. 44-B. No action taken.

Unit B lineages display recovery potential under stabilized environmental margins. Exudate rhythms show partial restoration, and shared-tissue regeneration begins in micro-filament form. Without intervention, volatility remains a limiting factor for full recovery.

Unit A lineages maintain aggression signatures, though metabolic reserves continue to fall.

Tension increases at the observer level, though no explicit statements record this directly.
End of Log.

DIRECTOR LOG — P6.S16.D

Summary Interval: Cycle 0199

Intervention constitutes a direct corruption of experimental integrity. The system's informational value derives from unaltered dynamics; external stabilization would eliminate the possibility of assessing authentic survival pathways.

Competitive survivors embody the authentic trajectory of life under duress: relentless escalation, cost-bearing endurance, and resistance to variance. Cooperative lineages, though capable of partial restoration, remain dependent on conditions they cannot regulate.

Maintaining non-intervention is essential for outcome validity.
End of Directive.

ETHICIST LOG — P6.S16.E

Cycle Reflection: 0199

Responsibility circulates here without being named. The Director's framing positions non-intervention as the neutral baseline, though neutrality is always a stance with consequences.

The request for intervention modeling suggests unease within the observer layer, but unease remains unacknowledged in formal documentation.

I record these shifts without declaring judgment, yet the act of recording feels increasingly insufficient.

End of Reflection.

DATAFRAG VI.Ψ — THRESHOLD PROJECTIONS (TRUNCATED)

PROJECTED GENERATIONS TO COLLAPSE (Unit A): 11.8
PROJECTED GENERATIONS TO STABILIZE (Unit B): 4.3
REQUIRED ENVIRONMENTAL BAND:
Lower Bound: 0.97 norm
Upper Bound: 1.04 norm

INTERVENTION MODEL:
Direct Biological Alteration: PROHIBITED
Stabilization Assist: UNRESOLVED
Baseline Definition: [REDACTED]

DATA_CORRUPTION: 18% packet loss.

FILE REF: INT/MODEL-PRED-Δ

Header indicates this file once contained preliminary intervention modeling for Condition Δ.

Only four lines remain visible:

Model suggests delay in action introduces non-linear risk.
Projected outcomes highly sensitive to timing.

--

Authorization withheld.

Redaction date matches cycle preceding the intervention vote.

SET 17 — PROJECTED FUTURES

ARCHIVIST LOG — P6.S17.A

TIMESTAMP: Cycle 0210.332 - 0212.998

Long-form projections completed for both evolutionary branches.

Unit A - Co-escalatory Branches:

Predictive models indicate collapse within approximately 12 generations.

For CREATURE-dominant trajectories, primary instability derives from runaway metabolic expenditure associated with increased armor density, toxin sequestration, and rapid-use extraction implements.

For PLANT-dominant trajectories, failure modes center on toxin overproduction, autotoxic drift, and defensive structure fragmentation where induced rigidity exceeds repair thresholds.

Across both domains, population oscillations narrow with each cycle, trending toward terminal decline.

Unit B - Mutualistic Branches:

Stabilization achievable under environmental bands narrower than current volatility levels.

For PLANT lineages, coordinated exudate timing and moderated structural growth reduce energy variance to within sustainable tolerance.

For CREATURE lineages, rhythmic intake adjustment and moderated access-tool use limit tissue turnover and decrease mortality from overexploitation events.

Within these constraints, survival and reproduction rates plateau at persistent values. Outside those margins, collapse remains likely but proceeds more slowly than in co-escalatory branches.

These projections were circulated to all observer terminals. No annotation accompanied the Director's copy. The Ethicist's copy was accessed twice.

End of Log.

DIRECTOR LOG — P6.S17.D

Summary Interval: Cycle 0213

Mutualistic future states are non-viable in scale. Their dependence on narrow environmental parameters ensures limited applicability beyond localized micro-conditions.

The co-escalatory trajectory, despite high projected collapse probability, represents an uncompromised demonstration of evolutionary pressure responses. Allowing it to run its course will yield complete data on maximal competitive escalation.

Intervention remains unjustified.
End of Directive.

ETHICIST LOG — P6.S17.E

Cycle Reflection: 0213

The phrase "letting it run its course" appears neutral but functions as a choice with a predictable end. Allowing collapse is still a form of decision, even if framed as passivity.

I attempt to phrase this as a methodological concern: that observational purity becomes indistinguishable from directed outcome when the consequences are known in advance.

The wording must remain technical. Anything else risks appearing as appeal rather than analysis.
End of Reflection.

FILE REF: GOV/INT-VOTE/717Δ

STATUS: Irretrievable

Log entry for formal intervention vote exists only as an index reference.
    Body content inaccessible.
    All attempts at recovery failed.

Reason for loss untraceable.
    Entry preserved in null state.

SET 18 —
DECISION THRESHOLD

ARCHIVIST LOG — P6.S18.A

TIMESTAMP: Cycle 0224.220 - 0226.900

Institutional tension escalates. Logs show repeated access to Protocol Query No. 44-B, though no author claims ownership. Internal timestamps suggest at least three distinct observer interactions.

A formal vote on intervention was recorded under Control Ledger Sequence 9-Δ, but the outcome field appears redacted at the system level. No metadata accompanies the redaction. It is unclear whether the omission is accidental or deliberate.

During the delay between vote initiation and the redaction, mutualistic populations showed increased mortality. Regeneration matrices failed in several clusters due to prolonged volatility windows. Co-escalatory branches experienced further attrition but maintained behavioral aggression.

Both trajectories now decline, though at differing rates.

DIRECTOR LOG — P6.S18.D

Summary Interval: Cycle 0227

Intervention would distort outcome legitimacy. To preserve the internal coherence of the experiment, all observer actions must remain detached from organism-level processes.

Co-escalatory dominance, despite attrition, continues to reflect the strongest adaptive vector.

Mutualistic lineages remain secondary—informative as alternative pathways but not primary models.

Non-intervention persists.
End of Directive.

ETHICIST LOG — P6.S18.E

Cycle Reflection: 0227

Delay now carries its own moral asymmetry. As mortality rises, the distinction between choosing later and choosing loss narrows. Yet the structure of these logs requires silence where concern would otherwise be expressed.

If the vote was redacted, the record has been shaped deliberately. If accidental, then omission guides interpretation nonetheless.

The threshold is crossed not when intervention occurs, but when its absence becomes irrevocable.

I can only document the moment. Its meaning will be determined elsewhere.

End of Reflection.

MEMO 6 — DIRECTOR PERFORMANCE REVIEW (REDACTED EXTRACT)

DOCUMENT ID: HR/Leadership-Evaluation/VX

Recipient: Executive Oversight Council

Subject: Performance Metrics for Director-Level Roles

Portions of performance review recovered:

- Director V.X. demonstrates "commendable consistency in outcome prioritization."
- Emphasizes "minimal deviation from projected competitive-path dominance."
- Shows "high alignment with institutional expectations regarding non-intervention purity."

Redacted lines indicate discussion on "potential rigidity regarding alternative viability assessments."

Final note (unattributed):

Outcome clarity preserved. Ethical conflict deemed non-operational.

—Administrative Review Board

PHASE VII
POST-DECISION ARCHIVE

MEMO 7 — ARCHIVE CLOSURE PROCEDURE

DOCUMENT ID: ARCHIVE/Closeout/717-Δ**
Recipient: Data Preservation Cluster
Subject: Final Storage Preparation

Initiate long-term retention protocols for Experiment 717-Δ.

- Compress non-essential logs.
- Retain SYSLOG anomalies without interpretation.
- Maintain redactions as-is to preserve archival authenticity.
- Cross-reference missing logs only by negative index markers.

Reminder:
Archival completeness does not require contextual clarity.
Preservation overrides coherence.

Submit verification upon completion.

—Archive Control Unit

FILE REF: COMP/LINE-FINAL/TRACE

STATUS: Degraded Beyond Analysis

File likely documented final indicators of competitive-line collapse.

Signal degradation pattern suggests unattended sensor failure.

Only timestamp remains:
CYCLE: 0238.550

No biological data preserved.

SET 19 — OUTCOME MANIFEST

ARCHIVIST LOG — P7.S19.A

TIMESTAMP: Cycle 0240.110 - 0243.991

Current mapping confirms the persistence of the cooperative/mutualistic lineage. Reciprocal structures remain intact across surviving clusters, though diminished in scale. Shared-tissue matrices show stabilized regrowth in low-volatility zones.

Co-escalatory/competitive-trajectory signatures no longer appear in reproductive tallies or metabolic scans. Behavioral markers once associated with aggressive extraction have tapered toward zero across twelve consecutive cycles.

Residual traces exist only as environmental detritus—isolated hardened membrane fragments without functional capacity.

No final collapse point can be identified.

Decline manifested as sequential reduction of viable clusters, decreasing in frequency until absence replaced pattern.

The archive contains no anomalies to account for the disappearance.

Only absence.

End of Log.

DIRECTOR LOG — P7.S19.D

Summary Interval: Cycle 0244

Outcome aligns with expected viability limitations of the co-escalatory trajectory.

Excessive metabolic expenditure, inflexible escalation, and resource-intensive repair cycles contributed to non-sustainability under prolonged volatility conditions.

The mutualistic lineage's persistence is evolutionarily consistent within constrained environmental bands.

Its continued existence does not invalidate earlier projections regarding its fragility; it merely indicates survival within a niche more forgiving than predicted.

Co-escalatory disappearance reflects non-optimal architecture.

No further analysis required.

End of Directive.

ETHICIST LOG — P7.S19.E

Cycle Reflection: 0244

Loss registers here not as an event but as a gradual thinning of the record: signals once dense now taper into unbroken silence.

The vanished lineage leaves behind no final gesture—only the outline of what no longer appears.

The surviving lineage carries no explicit memory of its counterpart; the archive must hold what they cannot.

Whether the silence left by the extinct is a remnant of limitation or a quiet rebuke remains unanswerable.

Its weight persists regardless.

End of Reflection.

DATAFRAG VII.° — POST-EVENT RESIDUAL

CYCLE: 0259.442
UNIT_A_SIGNAL:
Behavioral Markers: 0.000
Reproductive Index: 0.000
Structural Residue: trace only (<0.001%)
Trend: extinct

UNIT_B_SIGNAL:
Sync_Restoration: 0.67
Matrix_Integrity: 0.71
Volatility Sensitivity: high
Regenerative Pattern: probabilistic, sustained

SYSTEM_STATE:
Duality_Index: 1.00 → 0.00
Survivorship Condition: singular

SET 20 —
STABILITY AFTERMATH

ARCHIVIST LOG — P7.S20.A
TIMESTAMP: Cycle 0258.004 - 0260.770

The mutualistic lineage maintains stability within narrow environmental ranges. Shared-tissue regeneration occurs incrementally, with partial restoration of rhythmic exchange. Synchronization windows remain reduced but functional.

No co-escalatory lineage signatures re-emerge.

Chemical assays detect fading remnants of defensive compounds in substrate strata, degrading without replenishment.

Long-term projections remain sensitive to minor volatility.

The system functions, but with reliance on mutual restoration cycles and reduced redundancy.

Signals once associated with competitive interference—abrupt extraction patterns, toxin-layer ruptures—are permanently absent, creating a smoother but less varied data landscape.

End of Log.

DIRECTOR LOG — P7.S20.D

Summary Interval: Cycle 0261

The surviving system qualifies as sufficiently functional.

Its operational continuity depends on coordinated exchange and limited environmental fluctuation, constraining scalability but maintaining internal coherence.

System character—cooperative, synchronized, low-attrition—remains secondary to system continuity.

Preservation of a single functional lineage fulfills post-event viability metrics.

The absence of competitive traits reduces environmental stressors, further stabilizing the niche.

Outcome acceptable.
End of Directive.

ETHICIST LOG — P7.S20.E

Cycle Reflection: 0261

Continuity, while achieved, does not resolve the ethical tension underlying survival.

The lineage that remains persists through interdependence rather than dominance, yet survival alone does not define worth.

The absence of its counterpart renders the archive both clearer and poorer: a narrowed ecosystem preserved without its former contrasts.

What remains is what could endure—not necessarily what should define the system's future.

The distinction is not captured in metrics, but it alters the tone of the record.

End of Reflection.

SET 21 —
FINAL ARCHIVE
TRANSFER

ARCHIVIST LOG — P7.S21.A

TIMESTAMP: Cycle 0275.220 - 0278.004

Archival transfer initiated.

All surviving lineage data compressed for long-term preservation.

Shared-structure schematics and synchronization patterns catalogues under sustained-behavior indices.

Unit A lineage references preserved as null entries where relevant: blank matrices, inactive traits, collapsed branches.

Several regions of the archive contain gaps—missing logs, corrupted SYSLOG signatures, sequences ending abruptly.

These gaps have been retained without reconstruction, in accordance with preservation protocol.

As transfer concludes, the record feels simultaneously complete and diminished: a system reduced to a single trajectory, carrying the outline of the other only through negative space.

End of Log.

DIRECTOR LOG — P7.S21.D

Summary Interval: Cycle 0278

Experiment 717-Δ is complete.

Final summaries compiled:

- Cooperative-line survival trajectories
- Competitive-line extinction patterns
- Stability indices under residual volatility
- Long-term viability assessments

All essential data condensed into statistical archives for retrospective analysis. Non-critical logs and procedural documents sealed.

No additional commentary required.

End of Directive.

ETHICIST LOG — P7.S21.E

Cycle Reflection: 0278

This final entry remains brief.

Absence now dominates the dataset—not only the extinction itself, but the silences in the archive where earlier complexity once appeared.

Record-keeping continues, though meaning does not align itself.

The archive ends without finality, only with recognition that what survives and what vanishes share the same quiet in the end.

End of Reflection.

FILE REF: ARCH/ DRAFT-END

STATUS: Fragment Only — Never Logged Into Main Record

Recovered fragment:

...uncertainty whether record completeness equates to truth. Recommend—

Draft ends mid-word.
No evidence it was ever filed.

Recovered from secondary storage cache.

SYSLOG-CONT.CLOSE-02 — AUTONOMY SEQUENCE

CYCLE: 0278.900

SUBSYSTEM: Containment Unit B — Autonomous Maintenance

Observation channels deactivated.

Telemetry feed terminated.

Containment integrity maintained under default autonomous protocols.

Biological activity: ongoing.

End of SYSLOG.

END-STATE
RECORD — UNIT B

Final verification: biological signatures persist.
  No termination sequence located.
  No scheduled monitoring events.
  Record closed.

No further records are preserved beyond this point.

DOCUMENT ID:
TRFAM/GLOSS/717-
Δ

How to read Trait Reference Materials

THIS APPENDIX CONSOLIDATES terminology used through the 717-Δ observation cycle. It does not constitute interpretive guidance; it provides standardized definitions for recurrent descriptors across PLANT and CREATURE lineages.

Trait families are grouped according to functional domains rather than lineage classification.

Terms such as escalation-associated or stabilization-associated are used descriptively and do not imply intended directionality or value.

All entries reflect conditions observed within sealed containment Units and may not apply outside controlled environments.

Energetic metrics, variance indices, and fixation statuses represent cycle-averaged values unless otherwise noted.

These measures are included for internal consistency across analysis logs and do not serve as survival or viability predictions.

Users of this glossary should note:

1. **Trait families are emergent constructs**, developed from pattern clustering over multiple cycles.

2. **Terminology is retrospective**, created after initial divergence.
3. **No term denotes superiority or preferred trajectory**; all terms reflect adaptive outcomes within specific containment conditions.
4. **Cross-species parallels do not imply equivalence**, only structural similarity.

This document accompanies the Trait Evolution Tables and is intended for reference during comparative review of Unit A and Unit B trajectory materials.

Compiled for cross-cycle comparative analysis.

1. Defensive Morphology (PLANT)

Structural traits associated with modification of external or interface tissues.

Common Indicators

- Membrane densification
- Multi-layer reinforcement
- Toxin Reservoir formation
- Constriction responses

Functional Notes

Primarily affect boundary conditions between PLANT individuals and CREATURE contact points.

May increase survivability under direct resource pressure at the cost of elevated metabolic maintenance.

———

2. Toxin Handling and Reservoir Dynamics (PLANT)
Includes

- Synthesis of defensive chemical compounds
- Storage and multi-chamber reservoir development
- Regulated release during contact events

Functional Notes

Associated with escalation pathways.

Increase metabolic overhead proportional to complexity and volume of stored compounds.

———

3. Resource Access Morphology (CREATURE)

Structural or behavioral traits related to obtaining PLANT-produced resources.

Indicators

- Appendage mineralization/hardening
- Force-concentration geometries
- Precision-modulated feeding appendages (Unit B)

Functional Notes

Direction varies by Unit:

- High-force penetration in escalation trajectories
- Low-impact, calibrated contact in stabilization trajectories

———

4. Reflex Arc Modulation (CREATURE)

Neuromuscular timing traits governing initiation, delay, and rapidity of feeding responses.

Indicators

- Accelerated reflex arcs (Unit A)
- Delayed-initiation reflexes (Unit B)

Functional Notes

Controls the kinetics of interaction between CREATURE and PLANT surfaces. Affects tissue disruption, timing accuracy, and energy variance.

———

5. Exchange Timing Coordination (PLANT & CREATURE)

Inter-species synchronization traits governing the pacing and rhythm of resource transfer.

Indicators

- Exudate release cycling (PLANT, Unit B)
- Intake rhythm calibration (CREATURE, Unit B)
- Bidirectional entrainment patterns

Functional Notes

Stabilization families are defined by reduction in variance and increased predictability. Absent or disrupted in escalation trajectories.

———

6. Energy Distribution Patterns (PLANT & CREATURE)

Cycle-by-cycle partitioning of metabolic output across maintenance, repair, and reproduction.

Indicators

- Peak expenditure spikes (Unit A)
- Flattened expenditure curves (Unit B)
- Variance reduction metrics

Functional Notes

Highly predictive of long-term durability and mortality trends.

————

7. Structural Reinforcement Cycles (PLANT & CREATURE)

Processes through which tissues undergo periodic strengthening or repair.

Indicators

- Mineral turnover (CREATURE)
- Hardened tissue replacement (PLANT)
- Microfracture repair cycles

Functional Notes

Significant energetic burden; often associated with escalation-line fixation.

————

8. Interface Stability Traits (PLANT & CREATURE)

Traits affecting the amount of damage incurred during direct PLANT-CREATURE interactions.

Indicators

- Reduced tissue stress
- Decreased reflexive defense activation
- Precision-modulated contact mechanics

Functional Notes

Common in stabilization-lineage trajectories.
Improve survivorship and reduce energy waste.

---

9. Reproductive Filtering Mechanisms

Implicit selection dynamics that favor or suppress trait families based on energetic viability.

Indicators

- Decline of non-adaptive variants
- Fixation of high-cost traits in Unit A
- Fixation of low-damage traits in Unit B

Functional Notes

Not an active mechanism; emergent from differential survival under environmental constraints.

---

10. Variance Metrics (System-Wide)

Quantitative measures reflecting fluctuation in metabolic, behavioral, or exchange parameters.

Indicators

- High variance in escalation-lineage Unit
- Low variance under stabilized exchange
- Cycle-to-cycle fluctuation analysis

Functional Notes

Used for modeling long-term sustainability and collapse thresholds.

ABOUT THE AUTHOR

Matthew Dyer writes stories that linger in the quiet spaces between decisions, between people, between what is said and what is felt. His work spans literary fiction, speculative science fiction, and imaginative worlds, but is united by a shared fascination with perception, memory, and the small moments that quietly shape who we become.

He is drawn to characters navigating change without spectacle. Whether writing about a small-town bookshop, an experimental archive, or a fractured future, his stories favor atmosphere, emotional restraint, and the weight of ordinary choices.

Matthew lives in Texas with his family and works across creative, technical, and editorial disciplines. When he isn't writing, he's usually revising, designing, or thinking about how stories hold what we leave behind.